Most Charisma House Book Group products are available at special quantity discounts for bulk purchase for sales promotions, premiums, fund-raising, and educational needs. For details, call us at (407) 333-0600 or visit our website at charismahouse.com.

A GIANT ADVENTURE

Story adapted by Gwen Ellis

Published by Charisma House

Charisma Media/Charisma House Book Group, 600 Rinehart Road, Lake Mary, Florida 32746

Library of Congress Cataloging-in-Publication Data:

An application to register this book for cataloging has been submitted to the Library of Congress. International Standard Book Number: 978-1-62999-737-7

This publication is translated in Spanish under the title *Una aventura gigantesca*, copyright © 2019 by The Christian Broadcasting Network, Inc. CBN.com; published by Casa Creación, a Charisma Media company. All rights reserved.

19 20 21 22 23 — 987654321

Printed in China

"I can't do this," Chris whispered to his friend Joy.

"You have to, or you can never be in the band. You can do it—go on!"

"What if they don't like what I play?"

With that Joy gave him a gentle push. "Go on, Chris. Try."

A couple of minutes later a dejected Chris stumbled off the stage. "See, I told you I couldn't do it. Now I'll never get into the band. What can I do?"

Just like that, Superbook appeared and whisked Chris, Joy, and Gizmo, their robot, on a new adventure.

Superbook said, "I am taking you to see one of the greatest heroes of all time." And away they went.

"Where are we, Gizmo?" Joy asked. "And what time is it?"

"We are outside Bethlehem, and it is three thousand years ago. There are two armies nearby," the robot said.

"Armies? That might be cool," said Chris.

"Wait a minute," Joy said, scratching her head. "You were scared to play in front of a few kids and now you're going to join the army?"

When the three looked around, they saw a young man—a boy really.

"Who are you, and where are you going?" asked Chris.

"I'm David, and I'm taking food to my brothers who are soldiers in a battle."

"Can we come with you?" Chris asked.

"Sure."

After walking a while, they came over the top of a hill and saw the armies spread out below them in a valley.

Just then an ear-blasting shout rolled across the valley.

"I am Goliath. Come fight me, you cowards. What's the matter? Isn't there a man among you who will come and face me?"

"Why doesn't someone fight him? Why are you running away?" David yelled at the fleeing army. "Don't you know this is God's battle?"

Just then David's big brother Eliab came to him and said sternly, "What are you doing here, baby brother? This is no place for a child! We have no use for you. Go tend your flock, and leave the fighting to real men!"

"But they aren't fighting." David said. "They are running away. If they won't fight, I will!"

"Ah, kids," Eliab thought.

Just then Goliath's voice roared across the valley. "Who dares to come and fight me? Ha, ha, ha! What a bunch of cowards! Where is your God of Israel?"

"You don't have to fight Goliath," Joy reminded David. "You are just a boy, you know?"

"Yes, but I believe I've been chosen by the Lord for this very task," David told them. "Once, when I was with the sheep, a lion tried to steal a lamb. God gave me strength, and I killed it. Another time a bear threatened my flock. I grabbed it by the hair and killed it too."

"Oh, and then there was the time when I was called in from the fields and was anointed with oil by Samuel to be king of Israel. I felt God's power come on me as that oil ran down over me. I don't know how I'll ever get to be king, but I know it will happen because I have been chosen."

David gave a big sigh. "Yes, facing this giant is a job God has given me to do."

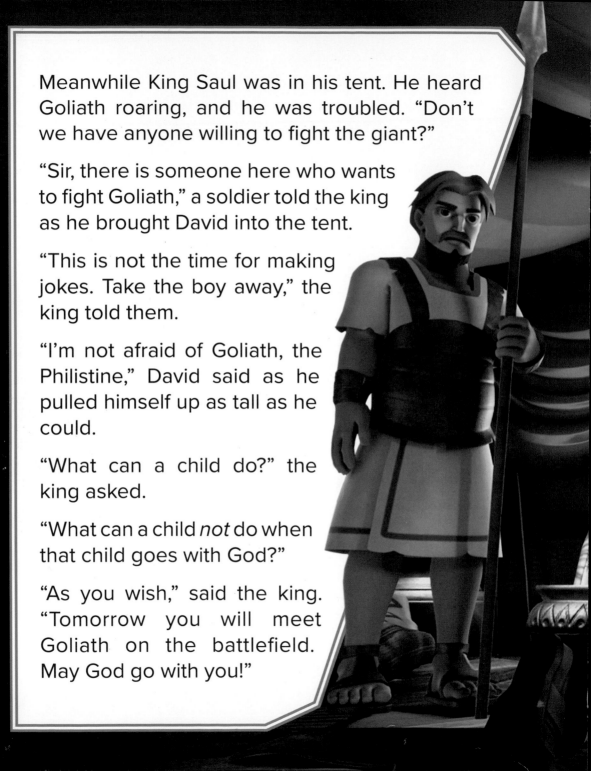

Meanwhile King Saul was in his tent. He heard Goliath roaring, and he was troubled. "Don't we have anyone willing to fight the giant?"

"Sir, there is someone here who wants to fight Goliath," a soldier told the king as he brought David into the tent.

"This is not the time for making jokes. Take the boy away," the king told them.

"I'm not afraid of Goliath, the Philistine," David said as he pulled himself up as tall as he could.

"What can a child do?" the king asked.

"What can a child *not* do when that child goes with God?"

"As you wish," said the king. "Tomorrow you will meet Goliath on the battlefield. May God go with you!"

Night came, and Joy and Gizmo lay down to sleep. Chris sat near the campfire with David, listening to him play the harp.

"That's pretty cool," Chris told David.

"Thanks. Do you play?"

"Umm, yes, but I'm thinking of quitting."

"Why would you quit?"

"I'm afraid people won't like the way I play."

"Who are you playing for? I play for God." David ran his fingers over the harp strings.

"I wish I had my guitar," Chris sighed.

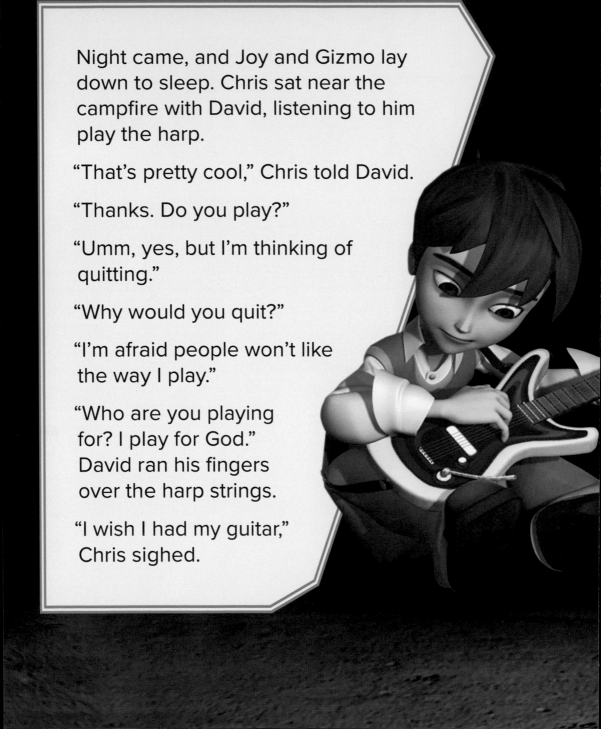

Whoosh! Gizmo shoved the guitar into Chris's hands, and Chris began to play a beautiful duet with David.

"You play as if touched by the Creator God Himself," David told Chris.

"Thanks. So do you," Chris answered.

"So, Chris, if God has given you the gift to play, you never need to be afraid to play for Him—anywhere."

Chris shrugged his shoulders. "Hadn't thought of that."

"Let me ask *you* a question," Chris said. "Why do you think you can beat Goliath when no one else thinks you can?"

"I know in my heart God is with me and He will give me strength when I need it most. It's like music. If you use your gift, then God will help you when you play."

"So the size of the giant doesn't matter, and the size of the audience doesn't either."

"Right!" David patted Chris on the back.

The next morning the king gave his own sword and armor to David.

"This won't work," David told King Saul. "I cannot walk with these."

"All right," said the king. "At least take my shield."

"Thank you, sir, but no. The Lord will be my shield." And with that David left the king's tent without any armor. He headed straight for a stream and picked up five smooth stones.

Now David headed to meet Goliath! Soon the huge, angry, mean giant arrived, and it was time to fight.

"This day the Lord will deliver you into my hand," David yelled to the giant.

"Come to me, and I will give your flesh to the birds of the heavens and to the beasts of the field," screamed Goliath.

"You come to me with a sword, a spear, and a shield, but I come to you in the name of the Lord of Hosts, the God of the armies of Israel." At that David took out his slingshot and quickly put a stone into it.

Whiz, whiz, whiz sang the slingshot as it whirled around David's head.

"Now!" David thought as he released the stone and let it fly...straight toward Goliath's head.

Kerthump! The stone sank into the giant's forehead and down he went like a collapsing tower.

David wasted no time and killed Goliath. God won, just as David said He would!

Before they could congratulate David, Superbook transported the travelers home—right backstage to the band contest.

"OK, Chris," Joy told him. "Go get 'em."

"God is with you," Gizmo reminded him.

Chris hurried to the stage, and boy, did he play! His playing was *amazing*! There was no question about it. He was in the band!

"You come to me with a sword, a spear, and a shield, but I come to you in the name of the LORD of Hosts, the God of the armies of Israel, whom you have reviled. . . . It is not by sword and spear that the LORD saves. For the battle belongs to the LORD."
—1 Samuel 17:45, 47